Maybe I should just quit while I'm ahead.

MILMOE 4 PREZ!

Don't be silly! We're walking right past this foolishness and we're hanging our posters around school as planned!

Hey, everyone, look! It's Hector!

I'm sure I can count on your vote, old buddy.

I mean, you're not really gonna try and run against me, are you?

Sweet eBeans! You have the latest ePad?!

Of course I do.

tap tap !

I camped out the night before they went on sale. Was the first in line. Here, take a look.

Whoa.

This must've cost a fortune! This thing is amazing.

Pfft! I still don't know what this school needs with a tech specialist.

I'm sorry, Orson, but no—I haven't seen your graphing-calculator watch.

C'mon, Hector, eat up! Lunch is prime campaigning time. We need to go table to table so you can start shaking hands!

Oh boy. And it's vegetable soufflé day. Can't we wait and campaign on taco day, when people are in far better moods?

Holy guacamole, Betty, there's a technology thief lurking in the halls of Thompson Brook! It's time to pull the plug on their operation!

I'll review this surveillance footage!

And I'll head into the halls to investigate.

But wait . . .

How will I communicate back to base without my Spork Phone?

Here, take this!

What is that?

It's a Crazy-Straw Earpiece. Place it over your ear and I'll be able to hear everything going on. It still has some kinks to work out, so I won't be able to communicate back.

But . . . you can still use it to sip chocolate milk.

Choco-lacto-licious!

Flying flapjacks! And I thought I had a lot on *my* plate!

Hey, Lunch Lady, remember what I said about keeping the cafeteria in order? The new superintendent just visited Shady River School, and it wasn't pretty.

Everything will be in tip-top shape!

Good! And, Lunch Lady . . . what is that in your ear?

After school . . .

BRRRIIOIINNG!!!

I did a search for copy shops in the area.

A1 Copy over on Russell Street prints large banners.

_click

Did you just call the first copy shop listed?

Was that who I . . .

Uh-huh!

Just pedal as fast as you can!

Well, I'll believe it when I see it. But in the meantime, I had an awesome interview with Orson.

What did you talk about?

With everybody's tech getting swiped, I figured the safety of the school is the most important thing. Because, bottom line—I want my X-Station Mobile back. I was really close to winning the latest Mega Mash Brothers game.

Well, you might be winning this election if you mash tomorrow's debate!

Guys, if Mr. Edison's cyborgs are still out there, what else should we be afraid of?

Hector, I listened to the podcast last night. You were awesome, my man!

Thanks! I just hope kids at school feel the same way.

They will.

THOMPSON BROOK SCHOOL

Hey, Hector, great interview!

Get up on the table and give the crowd what they want!

HECTOR!

My name is Hector and I want to be your school president!

We all deserve a safe, happy school! We won't be bullied out of this campaign!

HECTOR!

HECTOR!

HECTOR!

HECTOR!

Lookit our little green bean go, Betty!

He has my vote!

Too bad faculty and staff can't vote.

C'mon, guys, let's go pass out the Milmoe for Prez Frisbees on the basketball courts.

Lunch Lady, Terrence and I need to tell you something.

What's that, kids?

Last night, we saw Mr. Pasteur!

What? The substitute teacher?! Are you sure?

We're positive!

Can't be. That Mr. Edison is behind bars. Has been since we put him there!

And no Mr. Edison, no cyborg substitute. He's the one who invented Mr. Pasteur in the first place.

Here, kids, have an extra cookie. We're in the middle of an investigation.

The stolen tech?

You've got it, sassafras.

Today, we're setting a trap!

What is it, Milmoe?

Good luck today.

Huh?

I said good luck. I mean it. You've run a great campaign.

Thanks?

Mr. Milmoe, please step up to the podium. I hope you brought your speech.

Lunch Lady, look!

Well, I'll be! Gavin Computo, the tech specialist?! Let's go, Betty!

I know, my dear. It will be all right now!

But you've been stealing everyone's property, and that's wrong!

We're here to take it all back!

Nonsense! Once people get their computers and phones and games back, they'll all ask me to fix them! No more! This is my sanctuary, and I won't have you coming in and stomping on my dreams!

Your dreams?

Meanwhile, in the auditorium . . .

Remember, it is a privilege to vote in the school election.

Christopher Milmoe and Hector Muñoz will give speeches about why they should represent you as student body president.

Pssst!

First, we will hear from Hector Muñoz. . . .

Hector?

CONTACT!

Energy

It was a tight race, and in the end, the winner won by a handful of votes. And the next school president will be . . .

Christopher Milmoe!

It's an honor to meet you, Dr. Van Grindheimer!

Hmph.

FOR MY LICORICE-WHIP-SMART EDITOR, MICHELLE FREY

The author would like to acknowledge the color work in this book by Joey Weiser and Michele Chidester.

THIS IS A BORZOI BOOK PUBLISHED BY ALFRED A. KNOPF

Visit us on the Web! randomhouse.com/kids

Educators and librarians, for a variety of teaching tools, visit us at RHTeachersLibrarians.com

Library of Congress Cataloging-in-Publication Data
Krosoczka, Jarrett.
Lunch Lady and the video game villain / Jarrett J. Krosoczka. — 1st edition.
p. cm.
Summary: "Tech gadgets are disappearing left and right at school, and Lunch Lady must get to the bottom of it!" — Provided by publisher.
ISBN 978-0-307-98079-3 (trade) — ISBN 978-0-307-98080-9 (lib. bdg.) —
ISBN 978-0-307-98173-8 (ebook)
1. Graphic novels. [1. Graphic novels. 2. Video games—Fiction.
3. Schools—Fiction. 4. Mystery and detective stories.] I. Title.
PZ7.7.K76Lv 2013 741.5'31—dc23 2012025893

The text of this book is set in Hedge Backwards.
The illustrations were created using ink on paper and digital coloring.

MANUFACTURED IN MALAYSIA
April 2013
10 9 8 7 6

First Edition